Disney
Z·O·M·B·I·E·S
ZOMS vs. POMS

Adapted by
Bonnie Steele

Based on Disney Channel's Original Movie by
David Light and Joseph Raso

Zed is a zombie.

Zombies wear Z-Bands to stay calm.

He is excited to go to Seabrook High.

He wants to join the football team.

Addison is a cheerleader.

She is excited to go to Seabrook High.

She wants to join the cheer squad.

Her cousin Bucky is the captain.

Addison wants to fit in.

She has a secret.

She has white hair.

She hides it under a wig.

Zombies are sent to class
in the school basement.
They cannot try out for football.
They cannot join the computer club.

Zed sneaks out for football tryouts.
Someone sees him in the hallway.
She sets off an alarm.
Zed hides in a Z-Safe Room.

Addison hides in the room, too.
She meets Zed.
She has never met a zombie.
She thinks he is cute.

Zed keeps thinking of Addison.
He goes to football tryouts.
He cannot be on the team
because he's a zombie.

Addison keeps thinking of Zed.
She goes to cheer tryouts.
She makes the squad!

Bucky leads the first pep rally.
The squad's spirit sticks sparkle.
The zombies are afraid of fire.
Zed's friend, Bonzo, runs out
of the stands.

A cheerleader launches Addison into the air.

Bonzo knocks over the cheerleader.

Who will catch Addison?

Zed rushes to help.

Zed knocks off his Z-Band.
He now has zombie strength.
He knocks over the football team
to get to Addison before she falls.

Coach is impressed.
He thinks Zed can help the team win.
Zed says he will join if zombies
can have more rights at school.

Zombies can eat in the cafeteria now.
Everyone watches Zed and Addison
talk.
Someday this could be ordinary.

Zed gets tackled at the football game.
He asks his friend Eliza to help him.
She changes his Z-Band with
her computer.
Zed is stronger now.
The team wins!

Everyone is thrilled except Bucky.
Bucky doesn't like zombies.
He tells Addison to choose
between cheer and zombies.
She wants to be a cheerleader.

Zed helps the team win.
He helps the zombies fit in.

Zed invites Addison to a party.
It's in Zombietown.
He tells her he has been changing
his Z-Band.

Addison meets Zed's sister, Zoey.
She wants to be a cheerleader, too.
Eliza sees Addison isn't like Bucky.

It's past zombie curfew.
The police break up the party.
Addison gets caught.
The police take her home.

Addison's parents are not happy.
She tells them she was with a boy.
They want to meet him.

Bucky and the Aceys find out Zed
is changing his Z-Band.
They take Eliza's computer
to control Zed's Z-Band.

Zed shifts his Z-Band so
he doesn't look like a zombie.
He can meet Addison's parents.
His wrist hurts.
He can't keep doing this!

Zed is being someone he's not.
Addison wears a wig to fit in.
She is being someone she's not.
Something needs to change.

It's the championship game.
Addison leads a zombie cheer.
She is cheering for change.
Bucky kicks her off the squad.

Zed wins the game.
The Aceys turn his Z-Band off.
Zed turns into a zombie!

Eliza's and Bonzo's Z-Bands are off, too.
They turn into zombies.
The police take them all away.

Addison defends the zombies.
She takes off her wig.

She is different, too.
She gets booed by the crowd.

It's time for the cheer
championship.
Bucky cuts the squad down.
He doesn't want any zombie fans
on the squad.
The cheer doesn't start well.

Zoey joins the squad to help.
She doesn't care about being
different.
Addison and the zombies join, too.

Even Bucky joins the zombies.
They celebrate their differences.
They may not win, but they are in
it together!

DISNEY

Z-O-M-B-I-E-S 2

CALL TO THE WILD

Adapted by
Steve Behling

Based on Disney Channel's Original Movie by
David Light and Joseph Raso

Welcome back to Seabrook!
Zed and his sister, Zoey,
are zombies.
People used to think
zombies were monsters.

But not anymore!
Zed and Zoey can go
wherever they want.
They can even buy their
favorite zombie frozen yogurt.

Addison and her best friend
are going to cheer camp.
Addison's cousin leads
the Mighty Shrimp cheer squad.

He wants everyone
to be like him.
Addison is different.
She wants everyone just to
be themselves.

Zombies run the old
Seabrook power plant.
The town plans to tear it down.
Everyone is glad to see it go.

Well, not everyone.
Zed's best friend, Eliza,
says the power plant is an
important part of zombie history.

Zed has something special to do.
He is asking Addison to Prawn.
Prawn is a dance party, like prom.
This year, zombies can go.

Zed hangs a sign along the road.
Addison will see it when the bus
comes home from cheer camp.

But the bus doesn't see Zed!
He gets knocked off his ladder
and lands on top of the bus.
Luckily, Zed isn't hurt.

But the bus smashes through
a fence and off the road.
Addison and her friends
find themselves in a dark forest.

Addison wants to make sure
that Zed is okay.
She looks for him in the forest.
Little does she know
that she is being watched!

Suddenly, there's a loud howl.
AWOOOOOOOOOO!
Werewolves are in the forest!
All of Seabrook is afraid
of werewolves.

Zed asks Addison to Prawn.
She wants to say yes, but she
tells him that monsters can't go.
Seabrook's anti-monster laws
are back on!

That means no werewolves,
and no zombies, either!
Zed will find a way to take
Addison to the dance.

The werewolves think
Addison might be able to help
them find their lost moonstone.

The wolf pack shows up
at Seabrook High.
What will the werewolves do?

Everyone is ready for a big fight
with the werewolves.

But the werewolves don't want
to fight.
They just want to join the school.

Addison talks to the werewolves.
They tell her about the moonstone.
The werewolves need it to survive.
Addison wants to help them.

The werewolves invite
Addison to their wolf den.
She isn't afraid to go
into the forest with them.

The werewolves tell Addison
about a special person
who might save them.
Addison looks just like her!

The werewolves give Addison
a makeover.
Now she feels like one of them.

Zed and his friends are worried.

Where is Addison?

Did the werewolves take her?

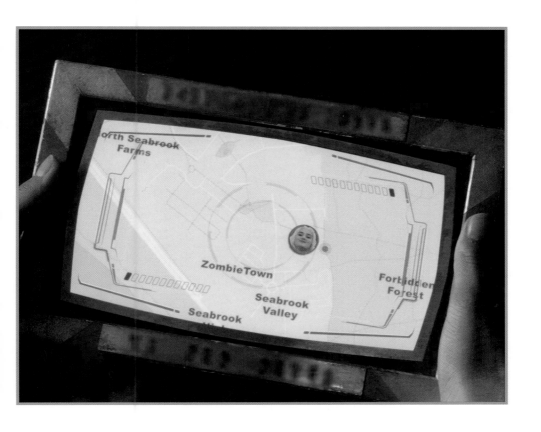

Eliza tracks Addison's cell phone.
The friends think the werewolves
might hurt her.
But they're wrong.
The werewolves want Addison
to join them.

Zed and his friends find Addison.
She thinks the moonstone is
beneath the power plant.
If the town destroys the building,
the moonstone might be lost!

The werewolves go to
the power plant to stop it
from being destroyed.
The Z-Patrol tries to arrest them.

Suddenly, Addison, Zed,
and their friends arrive.
They convince the town
not to destroy the power plant.

But something goes wrong.
The power plant is destroyed.
The werewolves think
their moonstone is gone forever!

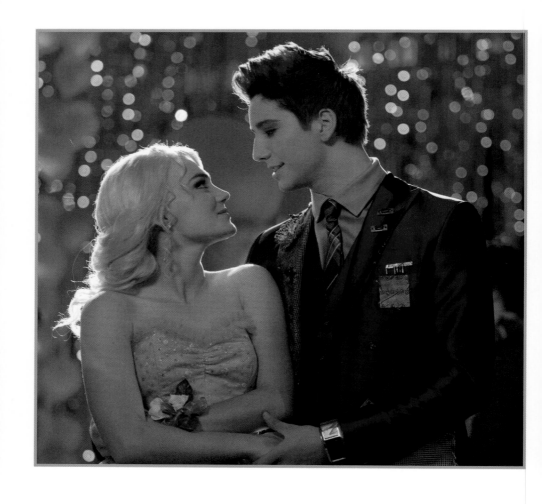

At last, Prawn arrives.
The humans, zombies, and
werewolves all go to the dance.

Suddenly, the ground erupts. Everyone joins the werewolves to search for the moonstone. Together, they find the powerful stone.

With the moonstone found,
the werewolves will survive.
And Prawn can continue.
All the kids dance, because
Addison brought them together.

DISNEP

ZOMBIES 3

OUT OF THIS WORLD!

Adapted by
Bonnie Steele

Based on the Disney Original Movie by
David Light and Joseph Raso

Zed is ready for the big game.
A college scout is here to watch.
Zed could be the first zombie
to go to college.

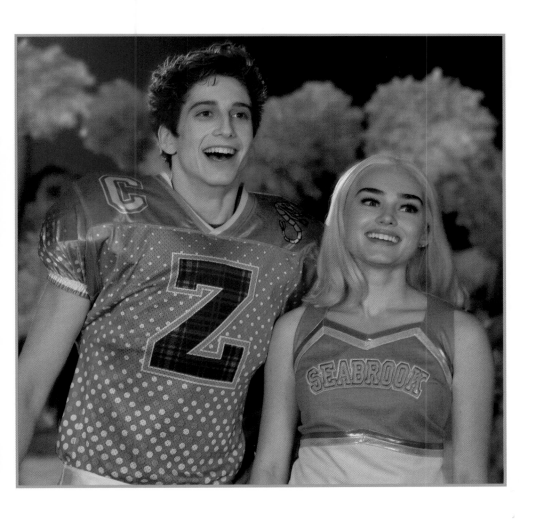

Addison leads the cheer squad.
She was already accepted to college.
She wants Zed to go to school
with her.

A spaceship appears in the sky.
Everyone runs to hide.
Aliens appear.
They come in peace.

The aliens must find their scout ship.
It has a map to their new home.
The map is hidden in Seabrook's
most precious thing.

Willa and her werewolf pack
don't trust the aliens.
But Addison welcomes them.
The aliens say they have come
to join Seabrook's Cheer-Off.

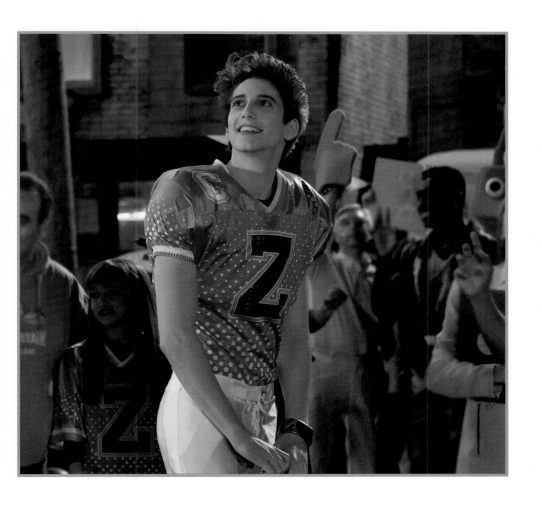

The college scout gets scared.
He leaves before seeing Zed play.
Zed is sad.
He still wants to go to college.

Aliens turn off their emotions. But A-spen wants to know about feelings. A-spen turns their emotions on. A-spen feels excited!

A-lan says aliens do not compete.
But he wants to know about
competition.
He finds winning fun.
A-lan enjoys competing with Zed.

The aliens' planet is gone.
They tell Zed about their map.
He offers to help them find it.
They will help him get into college.

A-spen feels funny.
Addison thinks they have a crush.
A-spen might love Zed!

The aliens visit the moonstone.
Is it Seabrook's most precious thing?
They scan it but don't find the map.

The werewolves arrive.

They must keep their moonstone safe.

The aliens hide.

They beam up to their ship.

Addison gets beamed up, too.
She sees Zed there.
A-spen invited him to come.

The aliens show them a message
from their scout.
The scout takes off her helmet.
It's Addison's grandmother!

Addison is part alien!
That explains her white hair.
She finally knows who she is!

But she doesn't have the stardust spark.
She cannot use alien tech.
She is sad.

A college scout returns
to talk to Zed.
Everyone comes to help him.
They want him to get into college.

Addison comes to support Zed, too.

She touches Zed.

There is a stardust spark.

It starts to turn Zed into a zombie.

Zed leaves the room.
Addison follows him.
Stardust sparks fly.

Addison really is an alien!

Zed is a zombie.

The college scout is scared.

The college scout leaves.
Zed may not fit in,
but he did his best.
Later he learns he got accepted!

It's time for the Cheer-Off.
The winners get the Seabrook Cup.
Is the map in this precious trophy?

The werewolves know the aliens lied.
They did not come for the Cheer-Off.
Zed tells the aliens to hide.

Addison and the cheer squad win.

They get the trophy.

They give the trophy to the aliens.

But the map is not in the trophy.

The werewolves try to stop the aliens.
They use their moonstone necklaces.
The spaceship gets damaged.
Why would Addison help the aliens?
She tells everyone she is an alien.

Addison's grandma used to say
Addison was the most precious
thing in Seabrook.
The map is in Addison!

The werewolves help fix the
spaceship with their moonstone.
Addison and Zed help, too.
The spaceship works!

Addison will go with the aliens
to find their new home.
Is this the last time she will see Zed?

It's graduation day.
Suddenly, a spaceship is in the sky.
Addison and the aliens have
returned.

Seabrook will be their new home.

Change can happen here.

You can be you in Seabrook.

Addison and Zed can go to college.
They can be together!